For Aunt Jane, with love
C. D. S.

To Toots and Paka
S. N.

Text copyright © 2002 by Carol Diggory Shields
Illustrations copyright © 2002 by Scott Nash

First edition 2002

Library of Congress Cataloging-in-Publication Data

Shields, Carol Diggory.
The bugliest bug / Carol Diggory Shields ;
illustrated by Scott Nash. —1st ed.
p.   cm.
Summary: All kinds of insects compete to see
who is the bugliest bug of all, but there is a
sinister surprise behind the contest.
ISBN 0-7636-0784-3
[1. Insects—Fiction. 2. Spiders—Fiction.
3. Contests—Fiction. 4. Stories in rhyme.]
I. Nash, Scott, ill.   II. Title.
PZ8.3.S55365 Bu 2002
[E]—dc21   2001025812

2 4 6 8 10 9 7 5 3 1

Printed in Hong Kong

This book was typeset in Alghera.
The illustrations were done in gouache and pencil.

Candlewick Press
2067 Massachusetts Avenue
Cambridge, Massachusetts 02140

visit us at www.candlewick.com

THE BUGLiEST BUG

Carol Diggory Shields   illustrated by Scott Nash

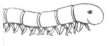

CANDLEWICK PRESS
CAMBRIDGE, MASSACHUSETTS

Do you have six legs?
Do you wiggle
or crawl?
Could YOU be
the bugliest bug
of them all?

A contest for insects!

News buzzed through the air.
Bugs slithered and swarmed
    from here and from there.

Down by the pond,
    young Damselfly Dilly
Said, "I'm a plain bug,
    neither clever nor frilly.

"But while I won't win
    I would still like to see
Who the Bugliest Bug
    turns out to be."

Fireflies lit up the stage
    with their lights.
Glowworms glowed softly,
    a beautiful sight!

A lacy white curtain
    hung from the trees
And billowed and swayed
    in the warm evening breeze.

The clearing was humming
    with bugs of all sizes,
Flittery, jittery,
    hoping for prizes.

There were more bugs than Dilly could ever have dreamed,
From tiny no-see-ums to fat termite queens.

Some had great pincers, some had proud horns,
Some looked like branches, or flowers, or thorns.

Dilly crept closer
    as the biggest judge grinned.
"Sweet little bugs,
    let our contest begin!"

"How odd," Dilly thought.
    "Those judges have wings
That are tied to their backs
    with gossamer strings."

Click beetles clacked, and whirligigs whirled,

Crickets sang solo, and swallowtails twirled.

A ladybug curtsied, tumblebugs flipped,

The judges applauded, then licked their lips.

The judges looked shifty,
   so Dilly kept squinting . . .
Then—sure enough—
   she spied their **fangs** glinting!

She yelled, "We've been
flim-flammed,
bamboozled,
distracted.
Those judges aren't insects," she cried. . . .

The big judge hissed softly,
    "Too late for you all—
It's curtain time now."
    And it started to fall.

"Folks," he continued,
    "we liked all your acts,
But we think we will like you
    much better as snacks."

The bugs froze in fear—
    this looked like the end. . . .

But Dilly thought quickly,
    and shouted out, "Friends!
There's only one way to
    get out of this mess—
Each insect must do what
    each insect does best!"

So—"Charge!" yelled a squadron
    of swift soldier flies,
And bombardier beetles
    took to the skies.

Dilly whirred up through
    a hole in the net.
"It's working, it's working!
    We'll beat those creeps yet!"

The army ants marched and

the mantises prayed.

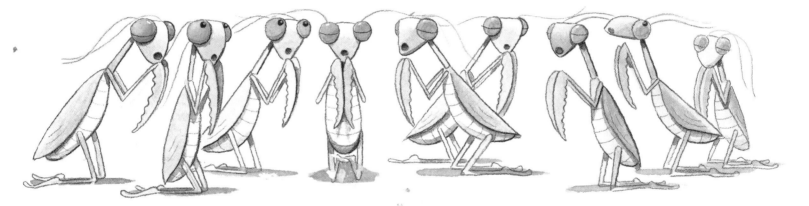

"Keep fighting," called Dilly,
"and don't be afraid!"

Then the stink bugs united, gave off their worst smells.
"P. U., we give up!" the spiders all yelled.

They scuttled away—

"Hurrah!" cried the bugs,
Giving high-sixes and
fuzzy, warm hugs.

The cicada piped up:
"It's time for a speech.
Attention, my friends,"
he said with a screech.

"The contest is over,
    and we have a winner—
Without this young damsel
    we'd all be dinner.

"She might be young and
    she might be small . . .